Scoop Saves the Day

based on the script by
Diane Redmond
with thanks to
Hot Animation

Simon Spotlight
New York London Toronto Sydney Singapore

Based upon the television series *Bob the Builder*™ created by HIT Entertainment PLC
and Keith Chapman, with thanks to HOT Animation, as seen on Nick Jr.®

An imprint of Simon & Schuster Children's Publishing Division
1230 Avenue of the Americas
New York, New York 10020

An earlier edition was published in Great Britain in 1999 by BBC Worldwide Ltd
First American edition, 2001

Manufactured in the United States of America

2 4 6 8 10 9 7 5 3 1

ISBN 0-689-84546-4

It was a wild and stormy night. All across town thunder crashed, lightning flashed, and rain poured down. By morning the storm had stopped, but a lot of damage had been done. Bob was the first person to hear about it.

"Bob! This is urgent," Wendy said, reading a fax aloud. "Roads are blocked and fences are broken. Immediate help is needed!"

"Okay, Wendy," Bob said, handing her his cell phone. "I'm on my way!"

Bob went out into the yard.
"We're needed right away," he said to the vehicles.
"I can dig it," chugged Scoop.
"I can roll it!" rumbled Roley.

Meanwhile Lofty, Muck, and Pilchard went to Farmer Pickles's farm to make sure everything was all right there.

"Look, we need to clean up the pond! C'mon, Lofty!" cried Muck.

While Lofty was piling garbage into Muck's dumpster, Pilchard decided to get a closer look at the ducks. She scrambled up the storm-damaged tree, and climbed onto a wobbling branch.

CRACK!

"Meow!" cried Pilchard, as she dangled over the water.

"Quick, Lofty! Do something! We've got to rescue Pilchard!" exclaimed Muck.

Lofty tried to hook the fallen tree, but he couldn't reach Pilchard.

"Chirp!" whistled Bird, and flew away.

"Look, Bird's going back to the yard for help," said Muck. "I'll go with him. You stay here and look after Pilchard."

Meanwhile Scoop and Bob were busy clearing a road into town.
"Left a bit . . . that's it. Well done, Scoop," said Bob.

“Help, Wendy!” yelled Muck, rolling into the yard. “Pilchard is stuck in a tree over the pond. And she can’t swim!” Muck said.

“I’ll call Bob right away,” said Wendy. “Oh, no! Bob didn’t take his cell phone!”

“One of us will have to go and get him,” squeaked Dizzy.

Across town, Bird found Scoop.

"Bird!" cried Scoop. "What are you doing here?"

"Chirp! Chirp!" Bird explained, hopping up and down. Scoop listened to Bird, wide-eyed. "Bob! Quick!" he called, swinging into reverse. "We've got to go!"

Scoop roared back into the yard.
"There's been an accident," cried Dizzy.
"A tree fell into the pond," Muck said.

“And Pilchard is stuck in the tree,” Wendy added.
“Lofty tried to lift the tree . . . but it’s too heavy,” Muck explained.

"Don't worry," replied Bob. "We're on our way!"
He turned to the vehicles.
"Ready, team?" he called.

"**Can we rescue?**" shouted Scoop.

"**Yes, we can!**" shouted everyone.

With their wheels turning as fast as they could go, they all set off for the farm.

Pilchard was very relieved to see Bob and the vehicles riding toward the duck pond.

"Don't worry, Pilchard," said Bob. "We'll have you out of that tree in no time! But first we have to move the ducks out of the pond so they don't get hurt."

Scoop picked up the ducks and gently placed them into Dizzy's cement mixer.

"Quack! Quack!" said the ducks.
"Oooh!" Dizzy giggled. "That tickles!"

"Now for Pilchard," said Scoop, and he gently placed his rear scoop under the frightened cat.

"Hop in, Pilchard!" called Bob.

Pilchard leaped off the branch and collapsed into Scoop's bucket.

"There you go," Bob said softly as he picked her up. "You're all right now."

Everyone was tired when they got back to the yard.

“Good job, team! Now let’s get a good night’s sleep,” Bob told the vehicles. “We’ve still got a lot more repair work to do tomorrow.”

When Bob walked into his living room, Pilchard was already asleep in her favorite chair.

"Purr, purr," Pilchard said, sleepily.

"Well, I'll be," laughed Bob.